Laugh-a-Long Readers™

JUMPIN' JUNGLE JOKES

by Diane Namm
illustrated by Wayne Becker

D0875149

New York / London
www.sterlingpublishing.com/kids

STERLING and the distinctive Sterling logo are registered trademarks of
Sterling Publishing Co., Inc.

Library of Congress Cataloging-in-Publication Data

Namm, Diane.
Jumpin' jungle jokes / by Diane Namm, illustrated by Wayne Becker.
p. cm. -- (Laugh-a-long-readers)
ISBN-13: 978-1-4027-5635-1
ISBN-10: 1-4027-5635-6
1. Jungles--Juvenile humor. 2. Jungle animals--Juvenile humor. I. Becker, Wayne. II. Title.

PN6231.J86N36 2008
818'.5402--dc22
2007030251

2 4 6 8 10 9 7 5 3 1

Published and © 2008 by Sterling Publishing Co., Inc.
387 Park Avenue South, New York, NY 10016
Distributed in Canada by Sterling Publishing
c/o Canadian Manda Group, 165 Dufferin Street
Toronto, Ontario, Canada M6K 3H6
Distributed in the United Kingdom by GMC Distribution Services
Castle Place, 166 High Street, Lewes, East Sussex, England BN7 1XU
Distributed in Australia by Capricorn Link (Australia) Pty. Ltd.
P.O. Box 704, Windsor, NSW 2756, Australia

Printed in China
All rights reserved

Sterling ISBN-13: 978-1-4027-5635-1
ISBN-10: 1-4027-5635-6

For information about custom editions, special sales, premium and
corporate purchases, please contact Sterling Special Sales
Department at 800-805-5489 or specialsales@sterlingpublishing.com.

How do jungle animals get to work in the morning?

They take a hippopota-bus.

What is a lion cub after it is three days old?

It is four days old!

What does a hyena call
a gorilla wearing ear muffs?

Anything it likes—
the gorilla can't hear it.

What's striped and goes around and around?

A tiger in a revolving door.

What do you do if a lion wants to sleep in your bed?

Sleep somewhere else.

What creature is yellow
with black and red spots?

A leopard with the measles.

What's as big as an elephant but weighs nothing at all?

An elephant's shadow.

Why do chimpanzees hide when they play cards?

The jungle has too many cheetahs!

What do you get when you cross a hippo with a mouse?

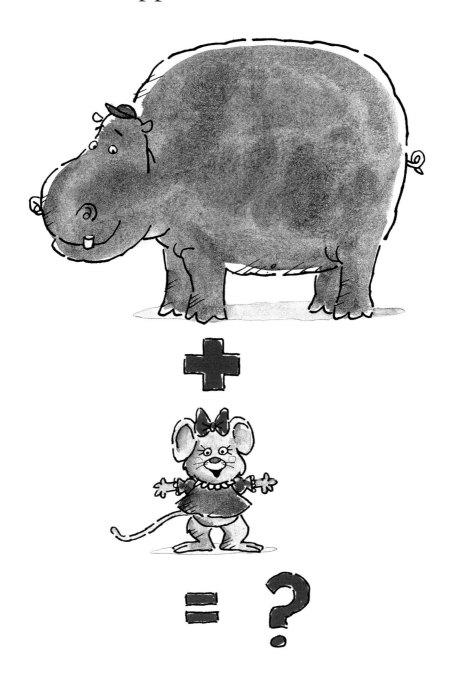

You get a hippopota-mouse!

What did the bumble bee say
to the Venus fly trap?

Hello, honey.

Where do frogs keep their money?

In a river bank.

What's bright red and weighs a ton?

An elephant holding its breath.

Why did the parrot cross the road?

It was the chicken's day off.

What's gray, has wings, and likes elephant teeth?

The tusk fairy.

What's black and white and noisy and loud?

A zebra on the drums.